This book belongs to

....

SANTA AND THE UNICORN

A Christmas Story

Orlando Quigly

*O*nce upon a time, there was a unicorn called Felicia.

𝓕elicia lived in a palace in the Kingdom of Mystica, set in the North-East of Fairyland. It was a wonderful palace, with lovely bedrooms with canopied beds. The kitchen was always spotlessly clean and polished. The windows were big and sparklingly clear, often with window seats.

When it was summertime, the glorious sunshine would stream through the windows and all the rooms in the palace were lit up with bright, golden light.

Now it was getting into the wintry season; the bare branches of the trees were blanketed in white and all of the unicorns were having great fun, racing across glaciers and having snowball fights.

The fairies from Fairyland would come round and play games together with them in the snow.

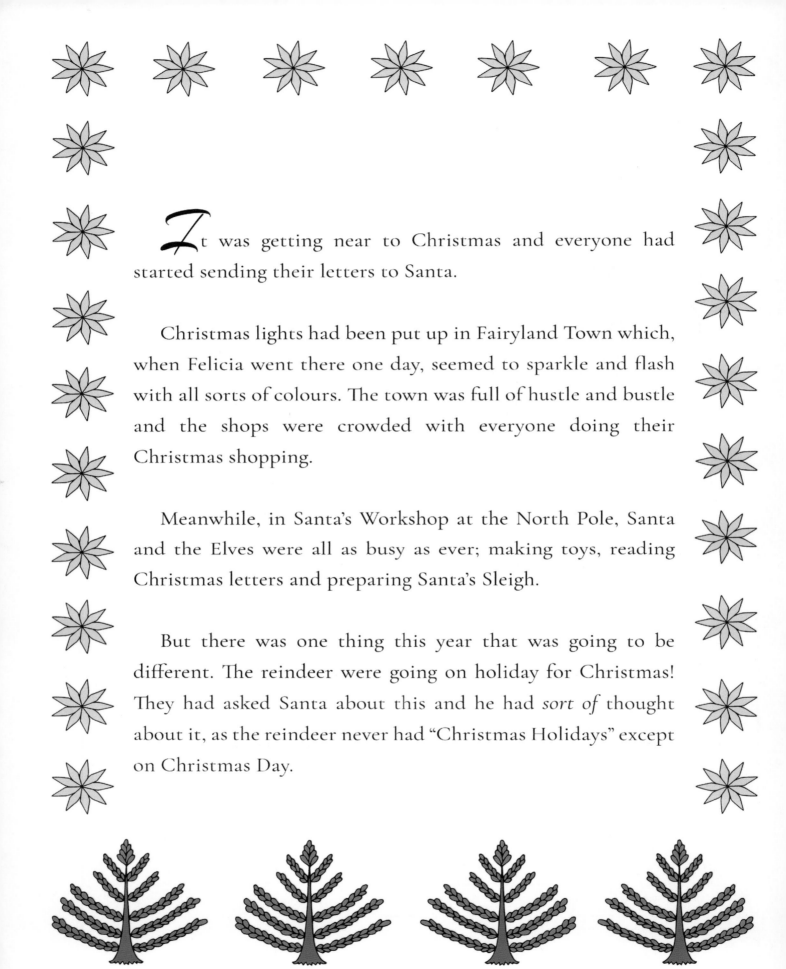

*I*t was getting near to Christmas and everyone had started sending their letters to Santa.

Christmas lights had been put up in Fairyland Town which, when Felicia went there one day, seemed to sparkle and flash with all sorts of colours. The town was full of hustle and bustle and the shops were crowded with everyone doing their Christmas shopping.

Meanwhile, in Santa's Workshop at the North Pole, Santa and the Elves were all as busy as ever; making toys, reading Christmas letters and preparing Santa's Sleigh.

But there was one thing this year that was going to be different. The reindeer were going on holiday for Christmas! They had asked Santa about this and he had *sort of* thought about it, as the reindeer never had "Christmas Holidays" except on Christmas Day.

*T*his was quite a discussion, until one day, ten days before Christmas, one of the Elves had a marvellous idea.

"What about if we Elves send letters to all the unicorns in Fairyland, asking if they can help pull the sleigh!" he suddenly exclaimed at the Discussion Table.

"What a good idea!" said Santa and all the other Elves. Just then, a reindeer came cantering into the room.

"Hello there!" he said in a Christmassy way. "Are we going to go on holiday this year?"

"Yes you are!" boomed Santa, "This Elf (here he pointed to the Elf that came up with the idea) came up with a marvellous idea, that we would send out letters to all the unicorns in Fairyland to ask if they could pull the sleigh!"

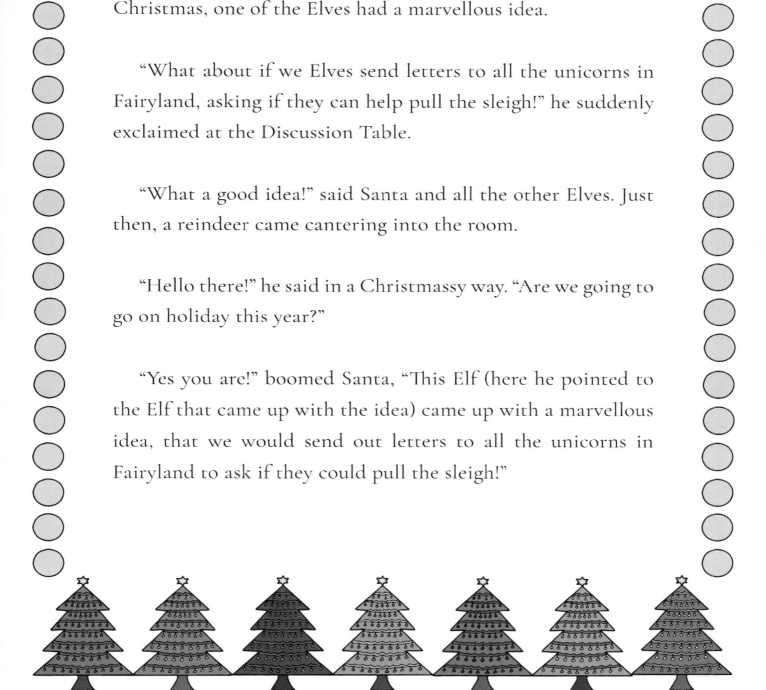

"Christmas Holidays!" said the reindeer in delight. "And are you coming, Santa?"

"I'm afraid I won't be able to come, my dear reindeer," said Santa, "but all the other reindeer can go with you, because we only need one unicorn to pull my sleigh."

"Of course," said an Elf, "one unicorn could easily pull a sleigh because of their magical powers."

"Hooray! The other reindeer are coming! What a marvellous idea, Mr Elf!" said the reindeer, and he plodded over to the Elf and shook his hand.

"The others *will* be excited!" he said, and off he went to tell the other reindeer.

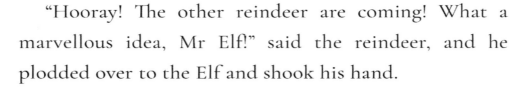

*T*he next day all the Elves were very busy writing letters to send off to the unicorns in Fairyland. That afternoon when they had finished, Santa went down to the village to post the letters.

"All of these to Fairyland please," he said to the people in the post-office.

So he got all the letters posted and came back to find the reindeer packing for their holiday. They all sounded very excited.

"Are you having fun?" Santa said to the reindeer in his booming voice.

"We are, it is so exciting. Have you sent the letters?" asked a reindeer.

"Yes I have!" replied Santa.

All the letters arrived at the unicorns' Kingdom the next day, while Santa and his Elves waited eagerly to hear back from them.

Over the next couple of days, the unicorns started sending letters back, about whether they could come or not. So the Elves were as busy as bees reading all the letters.

At the end of a day, that had been spent looking through all the letters, the Elves came into the Discussion Room and Santa asked, "Are there lots able to come?"

But the Elves shook their heads. "I'm afraid not," they all said together. "All of the letters are saying that the unicorns are AWFULLY sorry, but they are **so** busy this year, doing things for Christmas, and some are going off for a holiday."

"Are they, indeed," said Santa, calmly and peacefully. "Yes, well of course everybody's busy for Christmas. I'm sure the reindeer will be alright with that, anyway."

The next day the reindeer heard that they were not going on holiday, because the unicorns were too busy.

"Of course we don't mind at all," said the reindeer. "We're all happy to pull the sleigh, maybe next year they may be able to help."

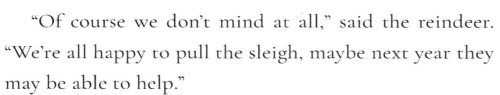

But that noon, when Santa and the Elves were sitting down for lunch, one Elf (who had not been at the table) came running in holding a dusty, scrunched up letter.

"Hello everyone!" he yelled excitedly, "Look at this!"

"What is it?" asked another Elf from the other side of the table.

"I found it in the Letter-Reading Room," said the Elf, "underneath the Letter-Reading Table. Somebody must have accidentally dropped it on the floor."

"What does it say?"

The Elf opened it up. "I haven't read it yet," he said. He then read out the letter . . .

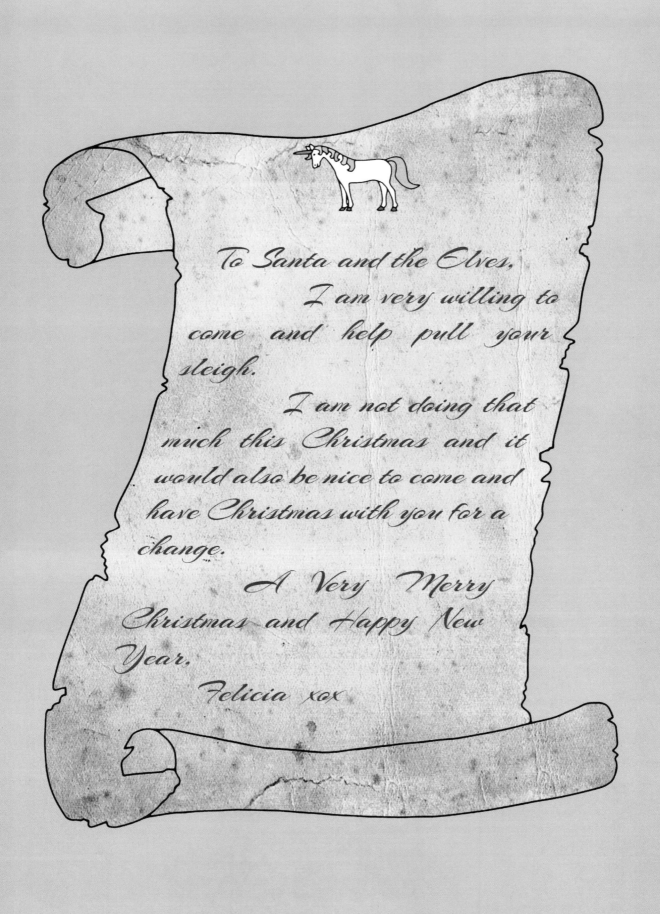

To Santa and the Elves,

I am very willing to come and help pull your sleigh.

I am not doing that much this Christmas and it would also be nice to come and have Christmas with you for a change.

A Very Merry Christmas and Happy New Year,

Felicia xox

"Well, Mr Elf!" boomed Santa when the Elf had finished reading the letter. "Aren't we lucky! One unicorn has got enough time to come!"

"How Brilliant!" everyone shouted. The reindeer were delighted that they could now definitely go on holiday for Christmas.

So, four days before Christmas Eve, Felicia travelled to the North Pole and arrived at seven in the evening at Santa's. When Santa and the Elves heard the door bells ringing, they immediately rushed to the front door.

"Felicia! She's here!" they all yelled, excitedly. Santa opened the door.

"MERRY CHRISTMAS!" boomed Santa, so loudly that Felicia, standing outside the door, jumped.

A couple of Elves jumped too, rolled out of the door and over, and over, and over in the snow, calling out, "Help, Oh Help!" until they were giant snowballs, before bumping into the Christmas Tree, picking themselves up, laughing and spluttering and throwing snow at each other.

Felicia, though, managed to stagger back to the door. "Oh, oh, Merry Christmas to you!" she said.

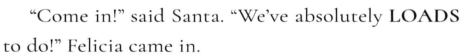

"Come in!" said Santa. "We've absolutely **LOADS** to do!" Felicia came in.

"It is warm in here!" she said, as one does after being outside where it is -30 degrees and then coming into a lovely warm place that's +20 degrees. Santa's house had very good heating in it, which they usually had turned off, but when guests who were not used to living in such a cold climate visited, they of course turned it on.

" *N*ow, Elves, we need to give Felicia a tour round my Workshop." So, the Elves gave Felicia a tour round Santa's Workshop, and Felicia, at the end of the tour, said how marvellous it was.

*T*hat night, Felicia slept in the best bedroom, but the others stayed up to do a little work; getting the presents ready to fill the sack and getting the sleigh and harnesses ready to set up for the next day.

Later, when the Elves and Santa were talking and planning, one Elf asked, "How is Felicia going to fly the sleigh? She doesn't have wings!" But this was going to be a fairly easy thing, as Santa had some *"Growing Wings"* magic that he would use.

In the morning Felicia awoke, and at first, upon seeing that she was in a different room and feeling a bit warmer then usual, didn't know where she was.

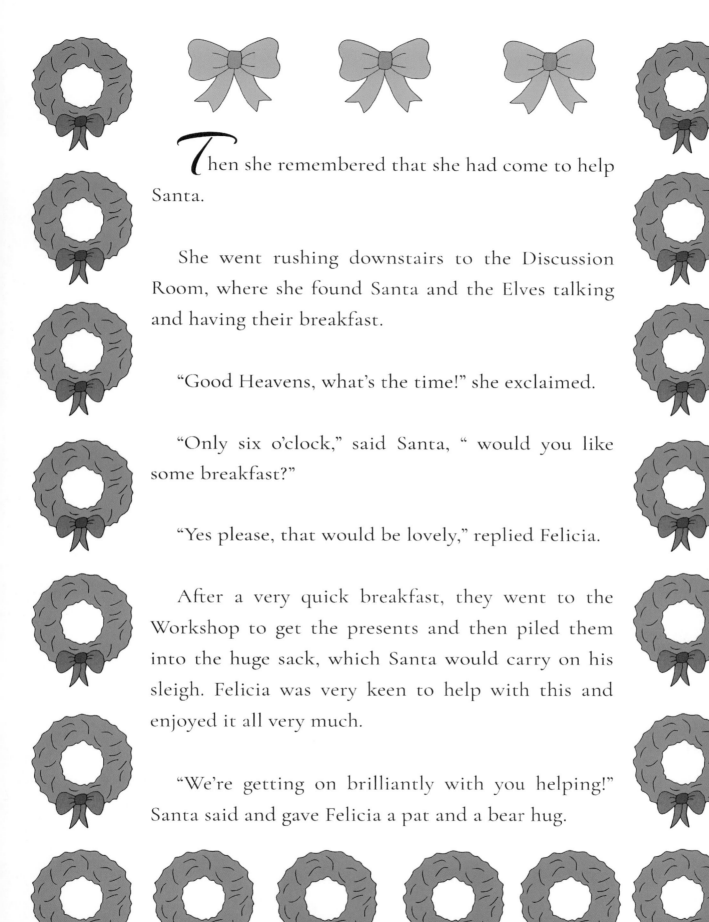

 hen she remembered that she had come to help Santa.

She went rushing downstairs to the Discussion Room, where she found Santa and the Elves talking and having their breakfast.

"Good Heavens, what's the time!" she exclaimed.

"Only six o'clock," said Santa, " would you like some breakfast?"

"Yes please, that would be lovely," replied Felicia.

After a very quick breakfast, they went to the Workshop to get the presents and then piled them into the huge sack, which Santa would carry on his sleigh. Felicia was very keen to help with this and enjoyed it all very much.

"We're getting on brilliantly with you helping!" Santa said and gave Felicia a pat and a bear hug.

Once they had packed the presents, they then needed to get the sleigh harnesses ready and that was simply all they really needed to do before Christmas Eve!

This meant that they actually had **TWO** days off, which they spent playing and showing Felicia around the North Pole.

*O*n the last day, they had to wake up fairly early as it was Christmas Eve - the day that Felicia was going to pull the sleigh! She woke up feeling very excited.

That morning, at the Discussion Table, when they were talking and planning merrily, suddenly Felicia said in an anxious voice, "How am I going to fly the sleigh? I don't have wings!"

"Well, we've got it all planned!" replied Santa. "I have got some magic that will help you grow wings! So no worries, my dear unicorn."

Felicia was quite relieved about that. The day was very busy, getting last-minute things ready. That night, when all the children had gone to bed and were fast asleep, it was time to use the wing-growing magic.

It was in a small emerald bottle and was the colour of a rainbow. Felicia thought it looked very beautiful.

"Now drink this," said Santa, "and you will grow your wings."

Felicia drank the rainbow coloured water. It was simply *Wonderful*. It really *was* similar to water but so fresh and clean and cool.

After she had drunk it, the unicorn looked round.

$\mathcal{S}$he was growing wings! Yes, she was, she was!
Felicia jumped around and about. She flapped her wings!
It was lovely!

 *S*oon they had got the harness attached and the sleigh was ready. The Elves were all outside ready to wave goodbye to Santa and Felicia.

"Are you ready?" said Santa. "Let's Go!"

 Felicia flapped her wings. Slowly at first, then faster, and faster, and faster, until, *yes*, she lifted off the ground, before circling around once.

They could hear the Elves calling goodbye down below. Santa and Felicia waved goodbye, before Felicia shot off forward, over the North Pole.

 They flew over snow-covered houses, across countryside that was completely *covered* in white, as well as big, bright cities that shone through the snow, stopping at all the houses and delivering the presents.

*E*verything was going very well, but when they were about half-way through, Santa's face suddenly turned anxious.

"Please hover for a second, Felicia," he said. He pointed. "Look yonder."

Felicia looked where he was pointing. Above them, the sky was moonlit and clear. But where Santa pointed, the sky was a dark, dingy black, that was heading their way. The landscape over there wasn't normal landscape, but pure white.

"There's going to be a snowstorm," said Santa, "and we've still got another half to complete."

"And, even worse, we're heading in the direction of it," said Felicia. "Of course, we'll have to carry on."

"Valiant Felicia," said Santa.

In a minute, the snow had started falling. It was light at first, but after another minute it was getting heavier and Felicia was finding it harder and harder to see.

After a few more minutes, it was almost impossible to see a few metres ahead.

"I hope we don't crash," said Felicia doubtfully.

Santa's sack was covered with snow, and he was trying to protect the presents inside. Felicia's horn had turned white and grown bigger, as it was covered with snow.

The snow was falling so heavily now that they could barely see even a metre ahead. Because of this they had to fly fairly low and stop every few metres to see if there was a house or not.

$\mathcal{S}$anta had his torch on full beam the whole time, but he could hardly see anything even with that.

"Careful, landing now," said Santa, beaming his torch down for Felicia. They were near finishing, but still had to fly back. Felicia lowered down, wondering where they were. Suddenly, Santa heard a little crack.

"Stop a second," he said, as loudly as he could. But it was too late. **Crash!** They heard themselves going through a row of branches.

A "Help! Oh Help!" was heard from Felicia. Another **crash** was heard. Santa held on tight to the sleigh. This time a big **crash** was heard and the sleigh tumbled upside-down. Santa held as tight as he could.

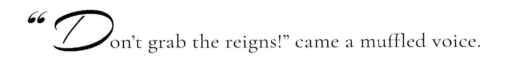

"*D*on't grab the reigns!" came a muffled voice.

Suddenly, "Where's the sack?" Santa said. And then everything went black. Another few **crashes** were heard. Everything was quiet for a minute or two. Not a word from Santa or Felicia. What had happened to the sleigh, the sack, Santa, Felicia?

All of a sudden, things became active again. The sky, which had been completely black, suddenly turned clear and full of stars. The moon came out and shone brightly. They were able to see properly at last. Santa and Felicia got up.

"What happened?" they both asked. Then they realised. Beside them was an immensely tall giant redwood tree. The sleigh was ditched in the snow, covered white.

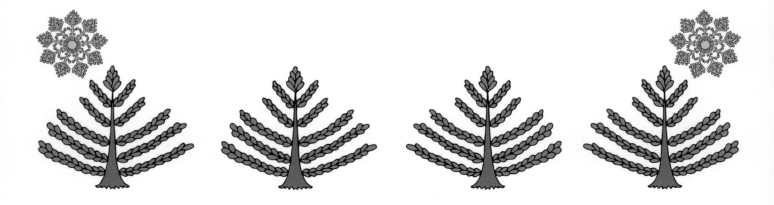

$\mathcal{T}$he sack had, unfortunately,
got blown away by the wind. The presents were lying scattered
round the field (they could of course see the bright wrapping
paper), and when Felicia looked, there was Santa beside her.
And when Santa looked, there was Felicia beside him.

 "I will go and pick up the presents," said Felicia.

"Thank you!" said Santa in his booming voice, which both Felicia and he were glad to hear again.

 Felicia piled the presents beside Santa in the sleigh. But they suddenly saw there was one more problem. The reigns were all messed up and broken.

"Oh dear," said Santa, "How *are* we going to fix that?"

 "Never mind," said Felicia joyfully, "I have some Super-Tape to fix those reigns! I'll just tape them up and they'll be as good as new!"

"Good old Felicia!" boomed Santa again. "Always prepared!"

 Felicia spent *just a few minutes* untangling and taping up the reigns. Then Santa strapped the reigns up to Felicia, and off they flew, up into the sky.

Santa checked his watch, *"A quarter to five! We need to be quick!"* Felicia zipped on, stopping quickly at houses and descending as fast as she could, then Santa rushed out of the sleigh and dropped presents off.

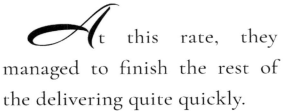

At this rate, they managed to finish the rest of the delivering quite quickly.

Now they started heading back, Felicia flapping her wings as fast as she could, so they were speeding on at a very fast pace. Soon they were approaching the North Pole. Before long, they could see Santa's house and tiny dots (which were Elves) around it.

Felicia slowed down her pace. Soon they were in a hover and started descending lower and lower.

They could hear the Elves calling,
"Welcome Back!" and "Great Felicia!"

Soon they had landed and were nice and warm inside Santa's house. The Elves polished the sleigh and a few went to make a new sack for Santa.

"What happened to your sack? Why was your sleigh covered in snow?" the Elves asked at the table that Christmas morning. Santa and Felicia poured out the whole story. "That was some heavy snow last night!" said an Elf.

The next day, Felicia woke up to bright sunshine streaming in through the bedroom window. She was going back to Mystica today.

That morning, at the table, when they had finished breakfast, Santa said, "Felicia, you have been so kind to help, I will give you this bottle." He handed the bottle that contained the rainbow-coloured water to Felicia.

She looked at Santa lovingly. "How *lovely*!" she said, "The growing-wings magic! You are so kind!"

"You are very welcome," replied Santa, "I hope you and your friends will have fun flying about together!"

A little later, at round about eleven o'clock, Santa and the Elves followed Felicia out to say goodbye.

Santa and his little helpers were all round, hugging Felicia.

"THANK YOU SO MUCH FOR HELPING US! YOU SAVED CHRISTMAS!" they all yelled.

As Felicia galloped away, she could hear Santa's and the Elves' voices fading in the distance.

The End

About the author

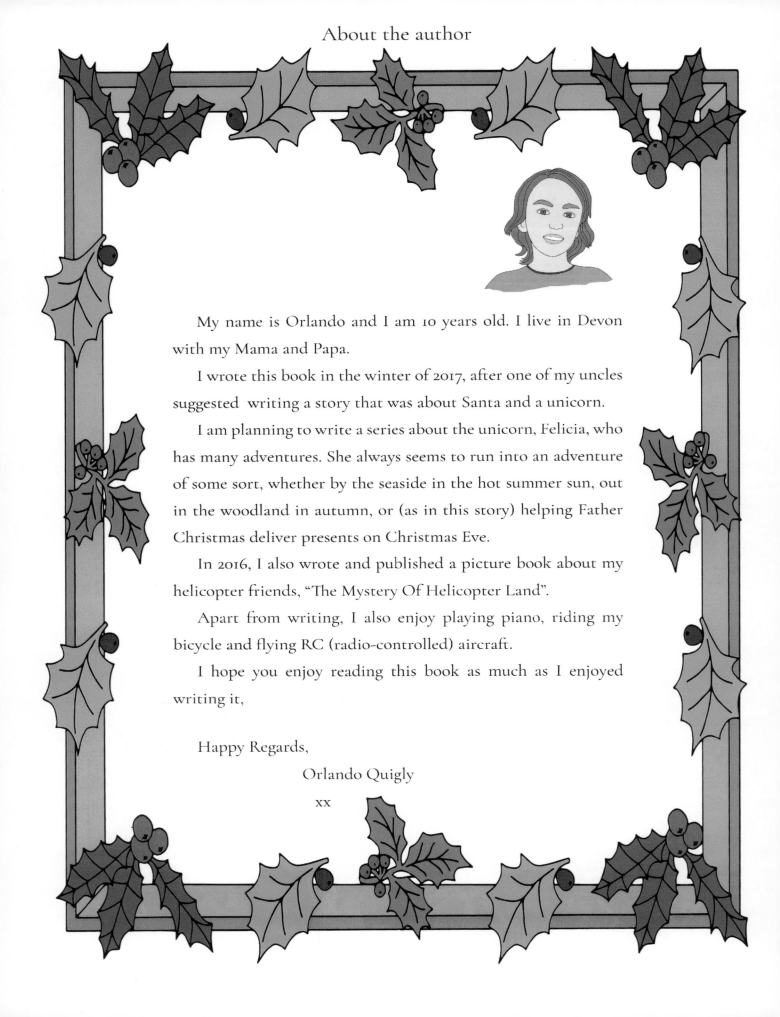

My name is Orlando and I am 10 years old. I live in Devon with my Mama and Papa.

I wrote this book in the winter of 2017, after one of my uncles suggested writing a story that was about Santa and a unicorn.

I am planning to write a series about the unicorn, Felicia, who has many adventures. She always seems to run into an adventure of some sort, whether by the seaside in the hot summer sun, out in the woodland in autumn, or (as in this story) helping Father Christmas deliver presents on Christmas Eve.

In 2016, I also wrote and published a picture book about my helicopter friends, "The Mystery Of Helicopter Land".

Apart from writing, I also enjoy playing piano, riding my bicycle and flying RC (radio-controlled) aircraft.

I hope you enjoy reading this book as much as I enjoyed writing it,

Happy Regards,

Orlando Quigly

xx

MERRY

Draw yourself, or stick a photo, here.

CHRISTMAS

Please visit the Artful Camel Books website if you wish to see what else we have to offer. We have published colouring books, for children and adults, including a colouring book version of this one.

We have also created T-shirts, available on Amazon, featuring Unicorns and more. There are personalised name shirts and designs to celebrate your birthday month or year.

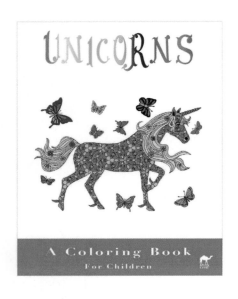

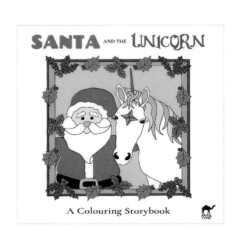

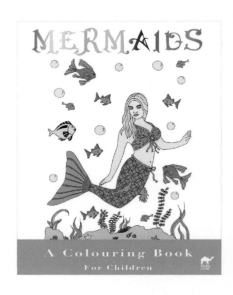

artfulcamelbooks.com

You can colour in this drawing if you wish, using colour pencils. It is a drawing from the colouring book version of *Santa and the Unicorn*, where you can colour in all the pictures to create your own unique copy.